USEFUL INFORMATION FOR THE SOON-TO-BE BEHEADED

Useful Information for the Soon-to-be Beheaded

Prose Poems by

SHIVANI MEHTA

Press 53
Winston-Salem

Press 53, LLC
PO Box 30314
Winston-Salem, NC 27130

First Edition

A TOM LOMBARDO POETRY SELECTION

Cover design by Kevin Morgan Watson

Cover art, "Wicker Basket" Copyright © 2010
by Lisa Valder, licensed through iStock Photo.

Author photo by Sam Grant

Printed on acid-free paper
ISBN 978-1-935708-78-0

For my grandmother, Ma (1928-2012),
the beautiful voice behind so many of these poems

and

For my loves—MMK, SMK, VK.

ACKNOWLEDGMENTS

Grateful acknowledgment is made to the following journals where some of these poems first appeared, in the same or slightly different form:

Coachella Review: A word for god, Letter to Grandmamma #1, Letter to Grandmamma #3, Letter to Grandmamma #8 (published as Dear Grandmamma #1, Dear Grandmamma #3, Dear Grandmamma #8); *Cold Mountain Review*: The Homecoming, The Dinner Party; *Fjord's Review*: The Collector, The Visitors, Anonymity; *Hotel Amerika*: The Horses of Sleep, Aftermath, The Museum; *The Prose Poem Project*: Requiem, Family Trait; *The Normal School*: The Blackbirds; *Used Furniture Review*: The Worry; *Generations Literary Journal*: The Scar; *Midwest Quarterly Review*: My Sadness #1, The Mutation; *Painted Bride Quarterly*: The Rock, The Butterflies.

Useful Information
for the Soon-to-be Beheaded

II

INTRODUCTION
by Tom Lombardo, Poetry Series Editor

I've been searching for a great prose poet to introduce to the Press 53 audience. Now, you hold the result of that search in your hands. Welcome to the prose poetry of Shivani Mehta.

Ms. Mehta lives in a realm where museums feature exhibits of various forms of wind, where men she adores live in her pockets—or her basement, where women's undergarments have the run of the house. In her many universes, butterflies, blackbirds, and mice populate worlds where the letter M might be interviewed on a celebrity talk show, where you might be trapped on an island with cannibals, where a gander may cook a ham and invite readers to dinner, where a severed head might retain sentience.

We learn what happens when the sighs of the dead have been captured for centuries and what happens to all those sighs when that custom is outlawed.

Prose poetry has been part of the canon for some time, despite the protestations of one or two poetically stunted academics. The French surrealists Charles Baudelaire and Arthur Rimbaud are generally credited with promulgating the genre, though there are earlier examples. The list of verse poets who've dabbled in prose poems is legion, and anthologies are full of prose poems by Amy Lowell, Gertrude Stein, William Carlos Williams, H.D., T.S. Eliot, Hart Crane, Ruth Kraus, W.H. Auden, Elizabeth Bishop, Czeslaw Milosz, David Ignatow, Robert Bly, James Merril, John Ashbery, W.S. Merwin, Mark Strand, Margaret Atwood, Frank Bidart, Robert Hass, Lyn Hejinian, James Tate, Mary Oliver, Maxine Chernoff, Richard Garcia, Rita Dove, and the list goes on and on.

But notably Charles Simic won the Pulitzer Prize in 1991 for his prose poem collection *The World Doesn't End*. Perhaps the poet most associated with prose poetry is Russell Edson who published several collections, including *The Rooster's Wife*, *The Tormented Mirror*, *See Jack*, and *The Tunnel* (Selected).

Shivani Mehta is both the heir to their trailblazing work and the next poet to pick up the baton and extend the race to prose poetry's future.

As you read her poems, you will note abundant attributes of prose poems, as espoused by noted poetry editors David Lehman, Michael Benedikt, and Peter Johnson, that come down to several keys in structure and style:

The obvious one—no line breaks. An intense use of tropes and sound, internal rhymes, and rhythms. The treatment of the sentence as the line, and the paragraph as the stanza.

Stylistically, prose poems tend to make the extraordinary seem somehow routine, to use staccato pacing, to involve macabre twists, to adapt unlikely models like news stories, memos, lists, parables, speeches, dialogs, obituaries, Facebook or Twitter postings. The prose poem disguises its true nature as a poem.

And the stories—ah, the stories! Ms. Mehta's poems are a riot of language, sound, cosmic shifts, mystery, and humor. They are poems of imagination, trope, and insight. And you will have great fun racing to keep up with them. This is a collection that you will not put down once you begin, so snuggle up in your comfy chair with your favorite libation and turn the page.

I

The Museum

I was thirteen the first time I visited the Museum of Breezes, with my Grandfather who was eighty-three. Housed in a stone mansion and founded in 1827, it boasts one thousand and seventy-three different species of breezes caught from around the world and categorized into sections by strength, according to the Wheeler-Yoshida scale.[1] The first section contains light summer winds, thin wisps of silk, clear and colorless in their glass jars stacked in even rows. In the slant of wintery afternoon light, the jars looked empty. I had to squint to catch the swirls before they vanished. The next section houses medium strength winds collected from cooler climates in the Northern hemisphere. These are wetter, like breezes after rain. Thick and murky, so heavy they sink to the bottom of their jars where they pool like grey mists in an open field. Grandfather said their stillness reminded him of the war, the time he crawled on his belly for miles, the weight of the sky pressing down like an old mattress. Lastly, cordoned off in a section by themselves are the storm winds, the squalls, gales, typhoons, hurricanes. These are the heaviest of all, thick and opaque, each imprisoned in its own shatter-proof glass cage, six inches thick to muffle their screams.

---

[1]The Wheeler-Yoshida scale for cataloguing breezes according to their weight was developed in the early 1800s by British meteorologist Mina Wheeler and Japanese climatologist B.C. Yoshida.

A word for god

I tell you how my voice cracks in dreams where I am a sea urchin washed ashore, waiting endlessly for the tide to take me. How, when I realize the waves that once taught me about the sea aren't coming back, I hurl my despair at the wind's nonchalance. Centuries ago the word for *god* was the same as the word for *storm*, the people wore amulets to protect against both. From my black inlet, I see the remnants of sacred objects—pieces of conch shells echoing chants, prayers, the leather thongs of ancient sandals, stone bodies of broken statues. Centuries ago men grew sons and waited while the women sailed in search of nameless catastrophe.

The Man

When I saw the little guy, nose pressed to the glass wall of his cage, I knew I had to have him. He was just what I'd been looking for, as tall as a ball-point pen when clicked open. He weighed no more than a sprig of black sage when I lifted him, placed him in the breast pocket of my shirt where he settled, nestled into the warmth of my body. I wondered if marsupial mothers felt like this, if they gestated their miniscule babies as I carried my little man, forgetting he was there until he moved, jabbed a hand or foot into the side of my breast. That first evening in my apartment we got acquainted over spaghetti and meatballs. I opened a bottle of champagne, poured him half a thimbleful. He ate five crumbs from my plate and a sliver of shaved parmesan the size of a clipped fingernail. I take him everywhere, dress-shopping, tucked into my waistband at the gym, on dates with other men. They never know he's there, pressed into my cleavage. At the office, I set him in a glass jar on my desk. He naps for much of the morning, sliding between the folds of an old dishtowel. Every evening, after supper I sit on the balcony, let him perch on my shoulder. *I'm so happy*, he murmured once, his breath teasing my earlobe, his fingers tickling my neck like a cat's whiskers.

The Horses of Sleep

The house we lived in was bigger inside than out. Corridors went on indefinitely, rooms rearranged themselves according to the weather. Often, the furniture disappeared for days, the antique chest in the hall scampering out the front door, followed more sedately by the dining room chandelier and pair of Rococo sconces.

My six brothers and four sisters lived in the other rooms of the house. I kept hoping I'd run into them but I never did. I always knew when they'd been reading Proust in the library—the words in the book had been shuffled round and some were missing altogether, an anemic shadow where they used to be. For weeks, I'd find solitary words all over the house—under chairs and caught between the bristles of brooms, discarded like used towels on the bathroom floor. Once I found two sentences: "One becomes moral as soon as one is unhappy" was pegged to a clothesline in the yard, sopping wet, next to white cotton frocks. "The horses of sleep move at a steady pace" was stuffed into the bread box, smeared with butter and orange marmalade, huge bites torn out. The scent of frying eggs roused me each morning. I'd leap out of bed and run down the rickety back stair, reach the kitchen just as the music of clinking spoons faded from the air. The stove sat as it always had, cobwebbed. Laid out on the kitchen table were a slice of bread and an opened can of condensed milk. I always ate these in bare feet, toes pressed into stone floor.

The Scar

Here's where I tell you I'll always remember the day, how five pounds ten ounces of tightly wrapped bundle pressed into my arms felt familiar. But this isn't about how I recognized your eyes, whiskey-brown like your grandmother's or your first hunger cry, frail for lack of practice. This is about how it all began with the slicing of skin, the sharpest point of the knife bearing down until the spill of red reflected in an overhead lamp. It's about how everything I know of love and its certainty I learned in that contact of blade and flesh. Most of all this is about the scar, raised pink line of fused skin that my fingertips trace in the dark.

Letter to Grandmamma #1

Dear Grandmamma,

It rained today and I remembered how you always said
thunderstorms brought news of old lovers. I am writing this letter as
I sit at our favorite restaurant, even ordered what we always did,
shepherd's pie and a pint of Killian's Irish red. It's been raining
everyday for a month. I find myself growing restless. Last night
when everyone was asleep, I stood on the deck in my nightgown
catching raindrops on my tongue. How perfect it looked, wet and
glistening. The rain seemed grateful I was there to taste it, to witness
its falling. I remembered how you always stood in the garden with
your face turned up when the sky hung low and heavy, like a cow's
laden udder. Last week I took a crowded bus to the museum, it
smelled of damp wool and cigarettes. I stood next to an old man on
the bus, our fingertips touching along the metal rail as water dripped
from the rim of his hat onto my pumps.

The children loved the candied fruit. They ate the whole jar in a day
and were sick enough to miss school the rest of the week. They say
to thank you and send their love.

The Butterflies

You unzip my dress, a curve from the side of my left breast to the
top of my hip. My body is a column of butterflies. One by one,
roused by the light and cool air, they wake from sleep. One by one
they open their wings, answering the instinct to be free. They scatter
in all directions; I learn what it means to be in many places at once.

Family Trait

My mother and I share the same hair, face, hands. Some days I get
the face, she gets the hands. Some days she takes the face before I'm
awake so I walk around without a hat, having no head to put it on.
Some days she eats her soup with a straw, having no arms or hands,
leaning forward for balance. At night we hang everything in the hall
closet—freshly shampooed hair, hands, face, all washed then draped
over hangers. We sleep in the spare bedroom side by side, flowered
nightgowns arranged over our limbs. Unable to see, we hear the
movement of stars.

Aftermath

The hole in the air is clearly visible when I get out of bed, blackness so complete it shimmers around the edges. Photographs of us are scattered through the house, broken glass under my feet like a trail of seashells. I know I won't find you. There are two kinds of people, you once told me, the kind who stay and the other kind. I smell rain in the kitchen, remember the taste of it on your lips—perfume of wet soil and inevitability. I've had a memory of your leaving since the day we met. The moon, its glimmer fading like an old lightbulb, swings by a rope from the fig tree.

Natural Selection

The twelve men in my cellar were collected at gas station. They're all likely candidates, a couple of lawyers, three teachers, a few accountants, even a handful of doctors. They've been down there for two days, there's a real sense of camaraderie among the men. I keep the cellar well stocked with whiskey, cigars, high-backed leather chairs. I admit I'm fond of one of the doctors, a cardiologist. We've talked things over; he's willing, he says, but only if I agree to let him have the second Sunday off each month. I let him kiss me after we'd settled things, let him slide his hands over my hips, up my back, his fingers splayed along my spine as if to trace each vertebrae. At his request, I undid the first two buttons of my blouse. He placed his stethoscope over my heart.

The Runaway

The last time my shadow deserted me, it ran off with all the clean napkins. When it came back two weeks later, thinner, the expensive white linens were crumpled beyond repair. This time my shadow has run off with all my silk scarves. I've searched in all the usual places, between the piles of old letters I saved, at the bottom of the swimming pool where it likes to float, in the cellar. Once, it sulked there for three days, eating chocolate and weeping, the crinkle of candy wrappers haunting my sleep. It's a frightful inconvenience, having to explain the absence of a shadow to people at cocktail parties. I've humored my shadow's every whim, even calling it *Henry* for a whole week when it asked me to, and *Lavinia* the week after that. I found a note on the kitchen table, balanced against the salt shaker. *I'm going where there is no sun, where I can see myself without you.*

The Debate

The televangelist my mother invited to dinner said, *I shall make the rain fall in straight lines*, and my mother said, *Pass the pickled onions*, and the televangelist said, *I shall make the rain fall and it shall be as disciplined as wooden soldiers on a chessboard.* My mother said, *Pass the fried chicken skins*, and this went on for a while. A man who could have been my father sat in front of the old television set, the kind with adjustable antennas. The televangelist said, *I shall make the rain fall in five minute intervals* and my mother said, *What about sex*, and her televangelist said, *It's people like you who are the problem*, and my mother said, *The kind you have with strangers when you think no one is looking*, and the televangelist said, *It's people like you* and this went on for a while. Somewhere an olive tree, tired of standing still, grew a littler taller.

Letter to Grandmamma #5

Dear Grandmamma,

Have I ever mentioned that my mother-in-law's hair often bursts into flames? Well, it does, with astonishing regularity. It did so again last night. She sat at the head of the table telling us about her recent trip to Yemen, when we noticed a strange smell, like burnt feathers. It overpowered even the aroma of Cook's Cornish hens. Then we saw that the top of her head was smoking. A few seconds later the first flames began to bloom. She looked beautiful. There was something regal in her bearing, the flames rose above her like the spokes of a crown, her parchment-colored cheeks flushed from the heat. That was when someone threw a glass of wine at the flames, which only made matters worse, not to mention how annoyed she was that her dress was ruined. In the end one of the dinner guests emptied the soup tureen over her. We tried to finish our dinner, but it was no use. Everything tasted like singed hair.

The children send their love. Yesterday Charlie fell out of the tree in our yard, broke his arm. He is delighted with the cast, and all the fuss.

The Pyre

Honoring the last wishes of her parrot, she laid the dead bird on a bed
of twigs and grass, set it alight with a match. Wanting to burn with her
companion of fifty-seven years, she stepped into the blaze; it enfolded
her, held her closer than any lover. For just a few seconds, the bird's
feathers glowed a brilliant green and the woman clothed in fire was
peaceful, more connected to life than ever in that instant before dying.
Over tea and crust-less cucumber sandwiches, a spectator said it was
like watching widows thrown on the funeral pyres of their dead
husbands, hair spiking flames, flesh peeling back like paper.

The Glass-eater

The best tasting are hand-blown glass birds in blues, greens, yellows. Not reds. I hold them up to the light to illuminate the pockets of space trapped between curved planes of glass. I like their shape in my mouth, rounded heads and tiny pointed beaks, protuberant bellies. I savor their weight, the nudge of wings inside my cheeks. My jaws flatten the delicate glass, not from any malice or ill-will. On the contrary, the closing of my mouth around each bird is affectionate, a welcoming home, eating beauty.

The Blackbirds

Wherever I went they were there, part of the landscape like trees, rocks. Even clustered outside the house. My mother came to visit for a week. She never heard the constant flapping, never noticed how their wings blocked the light. That was the summer I only saw the sky in jagged slivers, the summer black feathers turned up everywhere, in kitchen drawers and baskets of clean laundry. After my mother left she called to say a few feathers fell out of her suitcase, asked if I thought it was a sign. One morning I found sixteen dead rats outside the house. I called to tell my mother, *So what*, she said, *We all live in the shadow of something about to happen.*

The Labor

I'm trapped on an island with cannibals, only an axe to defend myself.
They come at me in a steady stream, expendable like light infantry or
pawns in a chess game. I close my eyes and swing, put all my weight
into it. When I open my eyes a head is cleaved in half, an ear lopped
off. Its like looking in a cracked mirror. An alarm clock goes off, the
strum of a heart beat. I wake and dress for work, put on a crimson
blouse, the hue of fresh blood pouring from a still warm body.

The Beloved

After the death of the princess, speculation was rampant as to the exact nature of her relationship with the pea, which during her life was kept in the royal chamber under a pile of one hundred feather beds. Some said the pea was a worthless charm given the princess by a peddler. But her chambermaids and ladies-in-waiting spoke in hushed voices of how the princess sang to the pea with every sunrise, her thick contralto filtering through stone walls and mingling with the stench of unwashed bodies, freshly slaughtered meat. What is best remembered is her devotion to the end, when the Royal Chamberlain decreed that the pea should be tossed out with kitchen scraps to feed the hungry. She chose death rather than witness the consumption of her pea, leaping from the tower window, her skirts wrapping around her like a shroud.

The Magistrate

Justice, justice shalt thou pursue.
—Deuteronomy 16:20

After the day's justice was dispensed, he was tired. The gray shutters
of his house were like tightly closed eyes. It was a house with white
gables, flowers outside the windows had exotic names, like the
women he used to sleep with. That was before, in his younger days,
around the time he spent nights drinking brandy distilled in his
kitchen, trying to nail splinters of moonlight to the bedroom walls.
Now of course, he made better use of his time. Most nights he was
down on his hands and knees, scrubbing dusk from the floorboards
like soot from a chimney.

Letter to Grandmamma #8

Dear Grandmamma,

Have you ever noticed how light filtered through glass on a wintry morning alters reality? I've been watching the new tenant of the house next door. He spends his days lounging in the courtyard in his dressing gown, singing Italian love songs. On Sundays he puts on pants and plays the violin. The young couple on the other side of the garden complained last week that he wakes their new baby. I watched the man today through the window, watched how the light grazed his face and bare chest, how it came in the kitchen at an angle and warmed my arms, my neck, my breasts under the thin cotton shift. And I thought how intimate it was that the same beam of light touched us both. Then the light shifted, everything blurred and was less magnificent. It was like looking out a car window through sheets of rain. Even his singing seemed louder and off-key, more sullen than joyful.

The children have been ill this week, Charlie's fever was very high and I thought of the fairy tale you used to read me, about dead children turning into constellations in the night sky.

Levitation

I'm sorry, my horse seems to have wandered through your bedroom window.
—Lady Godiva

I fell in love on the night train to Paris. It was around the time the toaster began to levitate, but what's a few inches above or below the spot where something should be. *Paris, I fell in love on the night train.* It took about a week for the toaster to reach the kitchen ceiling, where it hovered with the brooding air of a rejected suitor. *I fell on Paris in the night love train.* Then the coffee maker went the way of the toaster. It wasn't the first time, nor was it the first time I'd made love in an empty first-class compartment. Not the first time I felt plush velvet slide on bare skin. *Night fell in love on the train to Paris.* Not the first time, no, that the night took off her silk dress, let her lacy underthings slip to the floor. Not the first time the night said, *The trees look like old men.*

What We Gave Away

When I was a girl I used to be a tree. Years of therapy helped me look human, but now and then I hack off an arm or leg with a machete, watch a tree limb grow in its place. Some nights I sleep in the woods, branches furled around my body, leaf-tips grazing my skin. Last evening my sister came to rest on me. A butterfly, she spent summer evenings of her youth fluttering around the yard. There are photographs of family gatherings—me in dark blue dress with spaghetti straps, my branches bowed toward the gravy dish, she sipping from a champagne flute and hovering just above the rosebushes.

The Sacrifice

The sound of church bells followed her everywhere, a persistent chiming. People within a ten-foot radius heard it too. She was used to the looks as she walked down the street or went to the library, the furrowing of brows reminded her of sharp creases in folded paper. A few months ago a man on the street stopped, laid a hand on her arm. She tasted limes at the brush of his fingers on her skin. Speaking over the chimes he managed to tell her his brother once had the same problem and the only way to turn off the ringing was immersion in water. Best of luck, he said and walked away.

That night she tried it in her claw-foot bathtub, pressed her body into the water. She stayed under for a minute, two, five, reluctant to emerge for the bells were muted at last. She was prepared to die like this, drowned in her bathtub, imagined the cleaning lady would find her on Tuesday. Just before consciousness faded, tiny valves on either side of her neck began to open and close, bubbles escaping upward. Hours later, small flaps of skin grew between her fingers and toes. Eventually she gave up walking, her legs flattened then fused together, her body taking on the sleek line of a ship's streamlined prow. Now she lives by the sea, nothing but sand to separate her from blessed silence.

Requiem

I.

Wide open mouth of the baby waking from his nap in a soundless, frozen wail. White arcs of his crib, green sheets spattered with leaves. Time, stopped. Dishes in the sink that no one wants to do, scrambled eggs for breakfast, lunch, we usually skipped dinner. I take pictures of everything. Chipped blue bowl in the corner of the room, empty.

II.

The fire comes without warning, scorches acres. Sunset slides in over the windowsill, pools like smoke on the floor. Dark wood with swirls of blonde, her hair that summer we were thirteen. Outside the leaves crackle their burn-song. I watch them shrivel from the edges in.

The Emptiness Inside

Like good Italian pasta, human elbows are hollow. Osteopaths shake
their heads at this, insist that elbows contain things like bone, blood,
muscle. Our forebears knew the truth; the Babylonians, for instance,
spent decades documenting the hollowness of elbows, detailing their
findings in heavy tomes containing pages of drawings of
hollowness, emptiness so thick and viscous it leaked beyond the
boundaries of skin. In times of war, Babylonian citizens were asked
to donate the emptiness they all possessed, used by the armada to fill
the sails of their warships. They stood with raised arms braced
against the sea, hollowness flowing out with the tide, elbows
deflating like rubber balloons.

The Crash

She leaves one shoe, gold and strappy, in the middle of the bedroom but the place still has the eager blankness of a white canvas. She kicks it onto its side, the pale arch exposed, the under-belly of glamor. Good sex, after all, is just another kind of violence, the tangle of arms and legs like a plane crash. She remembers how, last summer, they bought a bag of tangerines and ate them sitting on the front steps, she savoring her's wedge by wedge, sweet or sour; he shoving half the fruit in his mouth at once, smashing the thin membrane, devouring joy.

Letter to Grandmamma #4

Dear Grandmamma,

There was a deer in the garden this morning. I watched it from the kitchen window as I sipped my coffee, waiting for the children to wake. The cup was warm in my hands, it snowed last night. The smell of fresh snow, the way it hung off the lowest branches of trees, reminded me of the winter we spent in St. Petersburg. The uncovered floor and freezing hallway of the small flat, its rough, uneven walls. Do you remember how I spent hours looking out the tiny window? How I held my breath each time someone walked over the thin ice of the frozen lake? Sometimes I imagined I heard cracks spearing over the ice, wondered what it would be like to drown in the lake's icy depths, if the slow freeze of bones might sound like wind chimes. And always, in the distance, cathedral spires rose through fog as though they floated above the earth. So much easier to believe in dead saints in a place where their sighs still echo in the air.

The children send their love, and want to know when you will visit. Charlie has a pet snake he dug out of a hole in the yard. I do hope it isn't poisonous. He's promised not to let it out of his room.

The Interview

M sat across from me on a suede armchair in his trendy downtown loft. I opened with the usual questions: How does it feel to be the 13th letter of the alphabet? What sets you apart from the twenty-five other letters? What did you want to be when you were young? What advice do you have for aspiring letters? M was very forthcoming, not at all what I expected after recent accounts of him as recalcitrant, even unfriendly. He confirmed rumors that the twenty-six letters of the alphabet have divided into two opposing factions. One faction, led by M, aims to unseat A as the first letter of the alphabet, replacing A with Z. "It's very difficult, of course," says M, "We're all very fond of A, she's done a wonderful job but its time for change." M also confirmed that he and S, his girlfriend of several years, have become engaged. When asked what attracted him to S, M said "I love her sibilance, the rush of air between the roof of my mouth and my tongue whenever I call her name."

The Flowers

Your mother sent me flowers on Valentine's Day . Strange, how it
always seemed to rain when she called, everyday for three months
after I left. *Marriage is forever.* After a while I knew who was calling by
the abrupt turn in weather. *Men can't help themselves when they see a pretty
girl.* A sudden stillness in the air gave her away—a purposeful calm
promising violence, the way the resting beak of a bird of prey
presages torn flesh, crushed bones.

The Yearning

My dream self likes to imagine she's a movie star in an old black and white, spends hours at her dressing table coaxing strands of hair into perfect coifs. Most mornings while I cook breakfast she's upstairs in the bedroom we share parading before the mirror in a flowing silk gown. Halfway through dinner she slides off her chair to the floor, imitating her favorite actresses, the ones known for fainting most adroitly onto the well-placed chaise or loveseat. She envies the graceful arcs of their bodies, the slow succumb to gravity. How faultlessly their lashes flutter, an arm flung overhead, how gaunt the point of an elbow, the taut line of a neck. At night I hear her running her fingers along the rows of gowns, the silk cascade caressing her hands, and she whispers, *someday, someday.*

The Hanging

The last thing he heard was a leaf detaching itself from a branch, like the tip of a green bean snapped off. The tunnel smelled like old blood and snow. He closed his eyes, heard the swish of his mother's gown when she danced a waltz. *I knew an old man who liked the scrape of stubble on his chin.*

Last

After the last forest had burned down, the last leaf fallen from the
last tree, I asked the cat, who was also the last cat, *What about dinner,*
and he said, *Artichokes in butter?* and I said, *Alright.* Then the last cat
brushed the dirt from my hair with a handful of straw, the way I
once rubbed down a horse, the last horse. The last boat, when it
came to take us across the river, commandeered itself because the
last captain was no more. The last mother and last father were gone,
I still mourned them at night under the last star. The cat said, *What
about dinner?* and I said, *I thought it was artichokes again* and he said, *we
ate the last one this morning.*

II

Anonymity

According to the six o'clock news, a five thousand dollar reward is offered for information leading to the safe recovery of Myra Jane Simpkins' missing torso. Ms. Simpkins is distraught over the loss of her torso, last seen by a ticket agent at the airport's international terminal. A reporter interviews Ms. Simpkins outside the bank where, she explains, her torso detached itself without warning. Sensing that something was amiss when she felt a sudden emptiness where her ribcage should have been, Ms. Simpkins turned around in time to see her torso getting into a taxi. As Ms. Simpkins speaks, a breeze begins to blow, flaps her blouse into the cavity at her midsection, allowing a glimpse through her. A man from the gathering crowd says that his mother once lost her torso but it turned up a few weeks later outside Graceland, having hitch-hiked all the way. There are support groups, the reporter says as Myra Jane starts to sob, psychiatrists who specialize in treating loss of torso. A recent photograph of the torso flashes on screen, described as "generally smooth and attractive, without distinguishing mark or blemish."

The Captives

In 1438 the dying were buried before they were dead, thirty seconds
before their eyes closed. To look at the faces of the dead was
thought to bring a lifetime of bad luck. The family of the soon-to-
be deceased stood by the freshly dug grave, waited to catch their
loved one's last breath as it slipped through a crack in the casket. The
youngest daughter was charged with catching the breath, which
sounded like a sparrow sighing when squeezed in the palm of a
hand. The breath was caught in a container shaped from the heart
of a willow tree, its edges sealed with wax. Breath-catching
continued for almost two centuries until abolished in the mid-1600's.
One evening in late summer, all captive breaths were set free. The
cacophony split the sky's curved dome. The night braced against
trillions of dusty sighs.

The Homecoming

There's a pair of African Grey parrots in my kitchen. I'm not sure
how they got there, but they keep me company at meals. *Hang up your
hat, Marvin,* one of them says. The other replies, *Three birds walk into a
bar.* They cackle like old women over a dirty joke. I was raised by my
grandfather, a shoe salesman who went door to door in a cheap blue
suit and red tie. When he died, I promised I'd keep up the tradition.
Yesterday I sold an expensive pair of ankle boots the color of butter
to a nun. I watched as she ran her hands over the supple leather,
trailed her fingers along the stitching as the plain gold band on her
left hand caught the light, her face reverent. She put them on the way
other women put on sexy lingerie. Only the toes of the boots
showed under her long, dark habit as she disappeared down the
street. One of the parrots said, *Did you see the woman from hell, the black
ash falling from the sky?*

The Mutation

I woke on a bed of nails again, the fourth time this month. The reason I've been going to bed in my thickest winter coat, I tell my roommate, is that I'm cold. But I know he's seen the white towels polka-dotted with blood, the ice packs in the freezer, flattened tubes of antiseptic ointment on the bathroom sink. After the last time it happened, I saw a doctor about my condition, lay on my belly in a hospital gown. He ran his fingers over the rows of tiny holes down my back, buttocks, thighs. He promised to run some tests, said he suspects it's genetic, the ability to transform mattresses into sharp objects in my sleep. Days like this remind me of the time I found myself transformed into a smooth pane of glass in a window, a red-breasted bird tapping against me with its beak.

Letter to Grandmamma #3

Dear Grandmamma,

Do you remember the summer I turned into an orange whenever anyone looked at me? It made people so uneasy, especially the teachers at school. When the other students began changing into fruit—peaches, bananas, pears, persimmons, I was sent to the principal's office. I waited while they telephoned you, each overheard phrase—"...not the first time...", "...disruptive behavior..."— made me more ashamed of my roundness. I tried to think of things that had nothing to do with my metamorphosis, like the satin of raw honey on my tongue, the unbearable pliancy, and I thought of the girl I'd read about in the Southampton paper who ran away on a train to France after turning into a grape, imagined I was her. I remember how the clock ticked, how a couple of flies kept me company, how your heels licked the linoleum as you walked down the hall. How you told me I was perfection, ripe and succulent.

The children are well. Charlie set fire to the bicycle shed last night, which I thought was very inconsiderate as we had guests for dinner. I sent him to bed without dessert even though we had his favorite, peach pie.

The Man in the Moon

My first lover was a gourmet chef. We moved in together, took food tours to Morocco, Fiji, the Maldives. For six months, he made me French toast each morning, with expensive caviar and freshly whipped cream. We ate together in bed, licking cream from each others' fingers, necks, earlobes. I ended it when I found him in the pantry in his underwear, his hand on a jar of homemade raspberry jam as though it was a woman's thigh, the narrow plane between her breasts. It took me three days to eat everything after he left, the puddings, pies, cakes, jellies, truffles, sautéed vegetables, braised lamb shanks in red wine reduction.

My new lover, the man in the moon, has a rugged, pockmarked face. I'd marry him except for his habit of eating clementines in bed after we make love, the sticky juice impossible to wash out of my sheets. In another month or two, I'll end it. I'll miss the texture of his skin under my tongue, the resonance of his moans in the dark.

The Worry

Convinced that the house would fall down the second the door slammed and she drove off in the taxi, Mother spent the morning stapling things together. She began by stapling the walls, then the floorboards, then the furniture was stapled to the floor. Even the petals of flowers were stapled open. When Father arrived home at six o'clock, she was just finishing in the kitchen. He'd hardly taken off his coat when she stapled him to his chair. She served him fried chicken and mashed potatoes with gravy, which he ate, staples and all.

The Garden

The gander in my garden cooked a ham, rang and invited me to dinner. I went, it would have been rude to decline. We tucked napkins into our shirts, ate with knife and fork. I admired the deftness of his wings, their skillful use of cutlery. We talked about the state of things, peonies grown wild and unchecked, the small broken bones of poultry strewn around us like seeds. When dinner was over I grabbed him and swung him round by the neck until it snapped, hung him from a hook in the meat cupboard with all the others. Tomorrow, I'm having tea with the goose.

The Children

When Mother came down to breakfast, she saw the children had sprouted wings again. They flapped haphazardly, careened around the chandelier which swung wildly back and forth. Mother recalled that the last time it took the children two days to come down. The children saw Mother and began to cry. "There, there, my loves," Mother said and took the plate of fried eggs and sausages from Father, shook her head at his face, red from exertion. Climbing a chair she held the plate up to the children. They stopped crying at once, began to eat with their hands, wings brushing Mother's ears. "There, there, my loves."

. .

The Keepsake

My mother had seven children, one for each time she was married.
I'm the youngest. She cooked ratatouille for dinner every night, with
seven loaves of bread laid end to end on the kitchen table. At seven
every morning my mother washed the thick inky curtain of her hair.
The scent of lavender still makes me hungry, still summons images
of fried snails, sweet yams. The night she died, a mocking bird
outside the window called my name seven times. This could have
been a dream. My siblings fought over her things—the antique silver
tea set, diamond earrings passed down from our great-grandmother,
mahogany dining table and chairs. I got her ashes, which I divided
into seven glass jars, the ones she used for strawberry jam.

My Sadness #1

My Sadness started fourth grade today. I packed it two sandwiches for lunch, one spread with marmite, the other with pickled anchovies, both with crusts cut off. I watched My Sadness walk to the curb, wait for the school bus with its lunch pail and backpack full of books with crisp pages, unbroken spines, no.2 pencils sharpened to points.

My Sadness has picked out its own clothes since it was quite young, not yet out of diapers. My Sadness likes to be wakened from naps with the brush of dead leaves against the soles of its feet. Most evenings it floats on its back in the bathtub, says it's the closest thing to weightlessness.

The Telephone

A telephone rings. No one answers. It keeps ringing. After a few minutes, the rings grow angry, disbelieving, like someone's betrayed lover. *Where were you? Answer me!* We cook a bird for supper, its wings tied, feathers in a heap on the floor. No one minds the blood, its expected, part of a balanced meal. The wind is lonely, it searches every dark street, tears the pins from women's hair. Someone carves the bird. I think of blood again, how it runs in rivulets just beneath the thin covering of skin. If only skin could travel like blood, go places, see the whole body. Blood has no belongings, owns nothing except its one purpose, to flow and keep flowing. The telephone rings. *Where were you? Answer me.*

Letter to Grandmamma #2

Dear Grandmamma,

Remember how you told me, years ago, that I was born from a handful of fishes? I'd like to know more. Was my mother a salmon, for instance? Was she beautiful, renowned for the unique symmetry of her pink scales? And my father, what was it about him that caught her fancy? Was it his agility, the way he flew over the water, skimming the tips of his fins along its glassy surface? No doubt it seems strange to you that I'm asking after all this time. There's something about aging, being surrounded by failures, moving closer to my breath slipping away. I find I cannot end without knowing my beginning. Perhaps I want to see the future. Perhaps I should have been a fortune-teller, like Great-Aunt Beatrice. Then I could begin all my sentences with *You will undertake a long and arduous journey.*

The children are well, and send their love. Charlie's arm is almost healed, and comes out of its cast next week. He is very disappointed.

The Visitors

Last night I was visited by the daughter and son I've yet to conceive. Both were disapproving of the company I've been keeping, the artist types who paint me, circling my belly-button as I let my limbs move to whatever is playing, like pieces of a scrambled alphabet. At first I thought they were just another pair of lost children, perhaps the neighbor's, but they called me *mother* and my womb—an organ I've never considered except to say what an inconvenience it is—began to hum. It started low, but each time they said the word, *mother*, it grew louder until my teeth shook and glass rattled in window panes. The humming continued after they left, a low vibration, the echo of footsteps in an empty room.

The Score

We hear the babies singing every night in their cribs. They always sing opera, their favorite is Verdi's *Aida*. We've considered telling people, asking the neighbors for help, but who would believes us? Last night we stood outside the closed door of the nursery, tried to catch them in the act. When they reached the high notes, we rushed into the room but the babies were too quick. They had stopped singing, eyes closed, faces innocent in feigned sleep. Sometimes while we fold the babies' clothes, clean up their spills, we say, *Come, babies, lets go out and play*. Or, *Why do you sing only at night, babies?* They only stare at us slack-jawed, drooling. We've thought about calling a specialist, a doctor with a background in conducting, a neonatal maestro, perhaps. We fall asleep listening to the blend of childish voices, tonight it's *Tristan and Isolde*. No one believes us, but we know they're snickering behind the nursery's closed door, waiting for the lights to go out. We hear the babies singing every night in their cribs.

Fertiliy Rituals of Eastern Europe, Part 1

In the village of Szlarky, outside Bucharest, limnick is held once a month under light of the full moon. A new mother is chosen to lead the dance, a coveted honor. One year, due to an unusually large crop of babies, they ran out of months. Six new mothers were denied limnick. There were complaints, a meeting held by Szlarky village elders. To keep the mothers happy, the elders decreed that limnick should be held twice a month. On another occasion, a man was caught spying on the women's ritual; masked women dragged him to a clearing and, following a short debate, gave him a choice: jump into the icy waters of the lake or couple with each woman. The following year, limnick was up from twice to four times a month. Those lucky enough to witness the ritual are changed forever. The dancers wear costumes of their own making, elaborate headdresses with animal hair and feathers, bits of tails, a few teeth. Moonlight grazes thighs and shoulders, breasts drooping with milk. They look like figures from the other side of twilight, nine feet tall with multiple limbs, like creatures who clawed their way out of the ground to stand upright and sway to wordlessness.

Medieval Professions: Corpse Carver

The entrance exam to the Corpse Carver's Guild was considered to be the most challenging of any profession, consisting of two parts and with only a 5% passing rate. Training started early, children as young as six were apprenticed to senior Carvers. As Carver's Apprentice they held picks and shovels, catalogued body parts. After a year or two the Apprentice, if she[1] showed any aptitude, graduated to the rank of Journeywoman and was permitted to do some carving herself. She began in the graves of children and the elderly, the bones being softer, easier to hack for the novice. For the veterans of the profession, the Grande Dames of Carving who wished to distinguish themselves further, there was the annual Carver's Cup—a race to reach the heart of a corpse first, with the least amount of digging and the fewest, neatest incisions.

Corpse Carving dates back to 1348, beginning shortly after the advent of the Black Death. The popularity of the profession at the time is attributed to the ease with which a corpse, or set of corpses, could be acquired by laypersons.

---

[1] Carvers' Apprentices were invariably girls during the profession's first hundred years. It wasn't until the late fifteenth century that boys were permitted into its ranks. Even then, Corpse Carving remained a largely female-dominated profession. (W.L. Grant, *Apprenticeship in the Middle Ages (1350-1499): A History* (University of Southampton Press, 1976)).

Useful Information for the Soon-to-be Beheaded

The following is an excerpt from a pamphlet designed by the Commission on Public Severance, handed out to condemned individuals as they waited in line for their turn at the guillotine. Reproduced here with permission:

1. Close your eyes tightly so as not to get dizzy when your severed head falls off the executioner's block and rolls across the wood platform, picking up splinters and human debris.

2. When you cease to feel movement, it is safe to open your eyes. Remain calm as you watch your body dragged off and stacked on a pile of headless bodies. Your head will be tossed or kicked into the basket of severed heads.[1]

3. This is likely to be the last time you will see your body. Expect a period of adjustment to the separation. You may experience a lingering sensation of movement in limbs you no longer have. This will pass.

---

[1] If the basket contains other heads, they will ease your transition. If yours is the first head in an empty basket, try not to think about the abrupt separation from your body. Focus instead on the details of your new surroundings: the closely woven fibers of the basket in which your head lies, the checkered spaces between the weave where sunlight passes through, the intermingled scent of sweat, tears, blood that permeates the air.

4. This is where your head will remain for whatever period of sentience it has left.[2] Your vocal chords will not work. You might begin to feel a sense of freedom, of lightness, buoyancy, like a balloon that is suddenly untethered.

5. Think back to the day you were born, remember what it felt like the first time light fell across your closed eyelids, the weight of air on your forehead. Remember the last time you were born human, the sensation of trailing your fingers in a lake, cupping water in your hands. Or, think of the time you were a bird, remember stretching your wings, pushing against the wind, taking flight. Remember that it always ends this way.

---

[2]On average, severed heads retain approximately fourteen seconds of sentience. However, exceptions have been known to occur. It has been reported that some severed heads remain sentient for several hours, and in a few cases, for more than a day.

The Dinner Party

I died in the middle of a dinner party and no one stopped what they were doing. They went on mingling and flirting, picking at hors d'oeuvres, stepping around my body as though it had always lain between the fireplace and coffee table. Even the cat, usually skittish around death, curled close enough next to me that I could have felt the warmth of his fur had I been still alive. Someone started dinner, I heard the sizzle of something in a pan—leeks in butter, I imagined—the pop of a wine bottle being uncorked, the pleasant drone of conversation. The shoes of guests moved in and out of my sight, sandals, pumps, open-toed, platformed with spindly heels no architect would judge to be structurally sound. The legs of women rose around me like slender trees, disappeared into their short dresses. It was the happiest I've ever been, surrounded by the hollows of well-turned ankles, the swell of calves, the pale vulnerability of inner thighs just above the knee.

My Sadness #2

My Sadness likes farfalle, pierces the center of each twist with a tiny hook, attaches them to the bedroom ceiling on long colorful threads. On Saturday mornings, My Sadness lies in bed, watches the swirls in the breeze, imagines itself in a cornfield surrounded by butterfly wings. My Sadness likes the sound of water dripping from a leaky faucet onto white porcelain. Most of all My Sadness likes to look out the window while munching on apples, eyes wide and unblinking, as if to learn the infinite patience of the sky.

Letter to Grandmamma #10

Dear Grandmamma,

I've spent the last two days of our seaside holiday gazing up at the clouds, their constant movement reminding me of a steadily revolving door. How easily they travel, no bags to pack, no schedule to follow. There is nothing else for clouds, no fortune they must seek, no destiny beyond their ceaseless migration.

Children run in the surf as I write, their narrow bodies as impermanent as the zinnias we planted in the garden on your last visit, the ones that died in the first frost of the season. Here, girls' voices are made of glass, memories of my girlhood are as thick as sails against the horizon. Chipped bathroom tiles under my feet, the anticipation of cold from under a blanket, bathwater warmed in a bucket with a submersible electric heater. The susurration of adult voices rousing me from sleep.

The children are having a marvelous time. Charlie wants to be a dolphin. I'm encouraging him to practice whenever he can.

The Festivities

In some parts of the world, eating *tse tse* flies while they're copulating is believed to enhance sexual prowess. I tried this once, on a dare. I remember what it was like to suck on the whirring of gauzy wings, how the frenzy of mating slowed, like everything else responding to the law of diminishing returns. Not everyone is born with five fingers on each hand, not everyone gets just two eyes. I knew a man with three eyes, the third buried in his left nostril. I have seen my father's vest clenched in my son's left hand. I have seen mountains roll over to expose their underbellies. Imagine the heat, the trumpets, the maddest among us submerging themselves in dust.

The Awakening

My palms on your chest, skin on skin. Steam from the shower
subdues the color of your hair, turns it grey. I am always loudest
when I know the upstairs neighbors are home. I picture them, an
elderly couple, with coffee, croissants, the morning paper as you
press me against the tiles and they etch into my back, feet arched
against a sense of falling. I am careful never to think of how you lie
about silly things, or how you are rude to wait staff. When I told you
last week that I'd decided to become a hummingbird, you wept but
didn't stop me. My wings thrum in the pink-tiled shower as I try to
breathe with my head under water.

The Caretaker

At the end of my street there's an old man who lives in a boot. He's been there as long as anyone can remember. He likes to ask questions of passersby. *Where are all the fig trees?*, he asked me one day. His favorite questions have to do with numbers, and falling. *What if you had only nine seconds left to live? What if raindrops were made of glass?* The drowning was a shock, its suddenness. On the Sunday before his body was found face down in the creek, the vicar came to call, the last person to see him alive. They said it was an accident, everyone knew he went skinny-dipping each night. No one disliked him, no motive was found, no marks on his body. The vicar was interviewed as a matter of procedure, asked to recall the old man's last words. *What if god has only two front teeth?*

Learning to Swim

My first husband collected the fortunes from cookies, kept shoe-boxes full of them. The fortunes he liked especially, he arranged in colorful crystal vases. He often went days without speaking, preferring to walk through the house silently reading fortunes as he found them. I became accustomed to quiet, to discussing with strangers intimate details of my life. *I'd like to have sex while crossing the Atlantic,* I once told the grocery checkout clerk, a young man with dirty hair, jagged fingernails. To pass the time I taught myself to swim in sand. It wasn't easy and I tired quickly, the sand pulled me deeper with each kick. The day I managed to swim half a mile in the sand I told my husband I was leaving. He plucked a fortune out of the nearest vase, said, *If you fall into a cactus bed, you'll be full of holes.*

The Adaptation

The Sun-Worshippers of Eastern Tibet are known as Nymarans[1].
Legend has it that the founder of the religious sect fell asleep in the
sun one day, waking with a sunburn. For days he writhed from the
burn covering most of his body, tended to by the local shaman.
When he began to molt, large patches of skin shriveling off like
parchment, villagers saw the shedding of his earthly skin as a mark
of divinity. Today the Nymaran monastery houses one hundred and
thirty-eight disciples, all men. They spend each morning offering
their bodies up to the sun, lying in even rows on the lush hillside. A
Norwegian anthropologist who recently visited the area observed an
interesting phenomenon: Nymarans are taller than the other
townspeople, going green around the edges and appear to have
developed the ability to photo-synthesize. On Sundays, the
townspeople come to watch the sunbathers, throwing flowers on
their glistening bodies and chanting prayers for salvation.

---

[1]From the Tibetan word *Nyi ma*, meaning *sun*.

The Rock

A rock the size of a house hovers outside my window. A woman sleeps in its shade. I try to open my window to warn, a rock is about to fall on her, but the window resists my attempts to open it. One summer my twin sister and I spoke only German to each other. Neither of us was very good but we always knew what the other was saying. We had long conversations, argued over which one of us was real, which one just the other's imagination. The woman sleeping under the floating rock wakes up. She looks at me, *Ich bin nicht diejenige die unter diesem Stein liegt; Du bist es.*

The Collector

She has them in every size, color, style, and fabric, collects them like some people collect stamps. 34As, 36Cs, DDs, 40Fs, reds, yellows, apple blossom pinks, frilly ones, underwired, push-ups, trimmed in scallops, black with white lace overlay like her grandmother's doilies. Sometimes she imagines a race of miniature people using the cups as parachutes. Lingerie overflows out of her basement, spills into the house and hangs from ceiling fans in every room, over the backs of dining table chairs. At dinner parties guests try not to look, gazing at the white tablecloth and place settings, blinking at the silverware polished to a reflective shine. But there's no ignoring the indigo satin C-cup with rhinestone trim arranged carefully between the potatoes and the mushroom soup, or the centerpiece—cherry-red silk demi with black lace trim. She tried, once, to explain—it reminds her of what she's lost.

Letter to Grandmamma #9

Dear Grandmamma,

I saw a mermaid in the pool last night as I strolled through the gardens behind the house. There was no mistaking the pearlescent glow of her skin in the moonlight or the fluid length of her, the shimmer of scales on flank and tail as she floated beneath the water's surface. It made me think of seagulls we saw at the beach in Maine a few summers ago, the effortless way they hung in the air without movement, riding the wind. Everyone says I should have asked her what she was doing in our pool instead of leaving out a dish of rampion seeds and stuffed olives. I remember you said that's what they like. After I went to bed I dreamed she was the sister I've always longed for, that she held out her hand.

The children are home from school for the summer. Charlie broke his other arm trying to fly from his bedroom to the tree house. I suspect he did it for the cast, I caught him admiring it in the bathroom mirror.

The Dress-maker

When my twin sister and I were young our mother was a dress-maker.
Beautiful dresses were all around us, dresses we weren't allowed to
touch, dresses made of crepe, cambric, calamanco, faille. At night we
wore nightgowns mother sewed us from old burlap sacks, once used
for fertilizer. We imagined how those other dresses might feel in our
hands, against our bodies, wondered if lace skimming up a thigh might
sound like the deliberate unhurried tearing of the thinnest parchment.
On our eleventh birthday, mother gave us each a pair of patchwork
wings, sewn from leftover scraps of fabric. With needle and thread,
she stitched the wings onto our backs. Our school uniforms had to be
let out to accommodate the wings which, even when folded, brushed
the backs of our ankles. I remember how my sister and I held hands
as we stood on the ledge of the attic window, how we soared into the
sky, how our wings knew what to do, how our mother's voice calling
for us to come back shrank to a tiny point like the volume on a radio
turned down too fast.

The Mice

They moved into the attic seven months ago, a family of fifteen. Aside from the aged Grúyère which every morning I find crumbled across the kitchen floor, they're the best neighbors I've ever had. Considerate, polite as freezing ice, they are careful to scuffle quietly and never have the music on after 9pm. Next week they're having a holiday party and I'm invited. I found the miniature invitation, printed on a grain of rice, pressed onto a page of my recipe book, between *Beef Stew* and *Duck à l'orange*. With a magnifying glass I read that the party is at 6 in the evening on Saturday next. Preparations are in full swing; a few nights ago I heard them dragging a Christmas tree up the stairs, the whole family—seventeen now, with the new additions—helping. Every night I'm lulled to sleep by the rustle of tissue paper, the *ping*ing of fragile glass ornaments, a restless chittering under the eaves.

The Notebook of Prophet

The Notebook of Prophet is hidden under a loose brick behind the outhouse. Its been in the family since the time of Great Great Grandmother. We women are the keepers, a sisterhood punctuated by cups of tea and cake served at the kitchen table. The Notebook of Prophet is present at births, marriages, deaths. It gets its own table. Sometimes, we take it out when we run out of things to burn, rip out a page at a time from the back. The front pages of the Notebook of Prophet we never touch. They are covered with curved shapes set evenly and close together, telling of things like the color of a mid-summer zephyr, or the exact location of heaven. Once, a villager set off to find it, carefully wrote down directions; he returned, maddened by what he saw, took to going naked on Tuesdays. They had to pry the Notebook of Prophet out of Great Great Grandmother's hands. Her last words were, "Imagine if our noses pointed up instead of down; we'd drown in the rain."

The Letters

I've always adored the letter *m*, its easy-going nature, how I can write it from left to right or right to left, the way my lips feel when pressed together to make the sound. When I was seven, I wallpapered my bedroom with *m* words cut out of the dictionary—*mangy, maggot, mallard, mandolin, multitudinous*. At meals I insisted on only *m* foods, macaroni, meatballs, mangos, marmalade and once, a whole jar of marinara sauce. Even my closet was full of clothes with *m* colors, *magenta, mauve, maroon, malachite*. Its been twenty-seven years, my therapist says its time to move on to the letter *n*, but I'm not sure I'm ready. Sometimes at night, I lie awake and try *n* words, roll them around in my mouth to learn their contours, their texture, their salty flavor like seawater—*nankeen, nascent, necrotic, neophile, nomenclature*. It's not the same, the *n*. It seems lonelier, more desolate, like its half of something.

The Reckoning

I once read that being in the presence of death is like watching
someone you love get on a train. There's that moment your eyes
meet and you both know its the last time. Its nights like these that I
have no regrets. Tying pigeons to trees is a prayer to stay death's
hand for one more night. What no one knows is, night is death's
lover. Night is everywhere, sliding up my legs, into the spaces
between my fingers. If I reached under the blanket I would feel
night's heat against my thigh, I would tell her things I've never told
anyone, how I still wake with the sensation I'm being buried alive,
dirt pressing my eyelids closed. How I dream that night's arms are
twined around my neck, her bones pressed against me as we dance.

My Sadness #3

When I heard My Sadness chuckling to itself, I knew something had to be done. For weeks I'd watched My Sadness grow happier, humming amongst the daisies when it thought I wasn't looking. My Sadness had forgotten who it was, lost its gauntness, grown ruddy-cheeked. I packed it off to Scotland, hoped a holiday might help My Sadness find itself. I got a postcard from My Sadness today. It's in Wales researching pagan legends, sketching the remains of old castles. My Sadness writes it wants to stay, that echoes of birdsong over stone ruins stir its memories of heartache. My Sadness writes that it has lost weight, that its grief grows stronger each day, more robust. My Sadness asks why it ever played tennis or swam, or let its hair grow so long it pooled at its feet like a black inkblot on a white page. My Sadness asks why it ever did anything other than lay on its back on an endless sea of grass. My Sadness asks, *Are you happy now that I'm gone?*

The Beginning of the End

The Beginning of the End wakes every night at 2.42. At 2.43 the first musical notes begin to play, bloom into an operetta that no one else hears, especially not the soundly sleeping man. The Beginning of the End tolerates wakefulness night after night, week upon week. Yesterday The Beginning of the End burned supper, burned it just short of inedible with the deliberate timing of a well-paid assassin. The Beginning of the End is familiar with the dark, its unbearable ache. One day, The Beginning of the End knows, the music will stop. Until then there's no good reason for the truth, that souls evaporate in the sameness of each day like drops of water in sunlight. Until then, lying is key to survival.

SHIVANI MEHTA was born in Mumbai and raised in Singapore. She moved to New York to attend college. A graduate of Hamilton College, she earned a Juris Doctor from Syracuse University College of Law in 2002. Shivani is the accomplished mother of toddler twins. Incredibly, they sleep long enough to allow her to write prose poems, many of which have even been published in various journals. She lives in Los Angeles with her husband, children, dog, two cats, and several fish.

A Note from the Author

I owe a debt of gratitude that I can never hope to repay to my mentor and friend, Rick Bursky, for his teaching, inspiration, generosity and friendship. Rick has the (dubious) honor of having read every word I've ever written. He believed in this book, and in me, from the start.

Tom Lombardo, thanks for 'finding' me, for your superb editing and faultless guidance. It was your oft-repeated directive to 'keep at it' that helped create this collection.

CPSIA information can be obtained at www.ICGtesting.com
Printed in the USA
LVOW07s0016020816

498685LV00002B/47/P